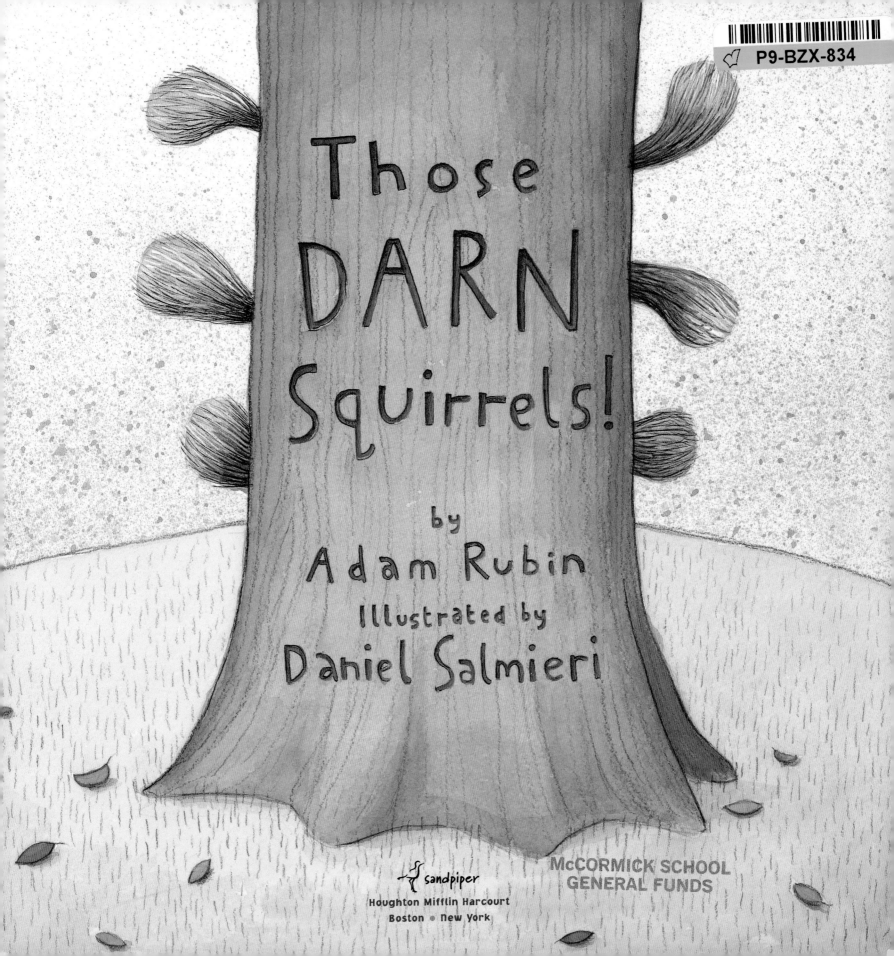

Those DARN Squirrels!

by

Adam Rubin

Illustrated by

Daniel Salmieri

sandpiper

Houghton Mifflin Harcourt
Boston ● New York

To my father, for his love of backyard bird
watching and Breakstone brand dairy products,
and to my mother, who sleeps like a horse
—A.R.

To Dad and Orla, for all your support
—D.S.

And, of course, to Corey—let's go Mets!
—A.R. & D.S.

The text of this book is set in 17-point Jacoby ICG Light.
The illustrations are watercolor, gouache, and colored pencil.

The Library of Congress has cataloged the hardcover edition as follows:
Rubin, Adam, 1983–
Those darn squirrels! / by Adam Rubin ; illustrated by Daniel Salmieri.
p. cm.
Summary: When grumpy Old Man Fookwire builds feeders to try to keep birds—the only creatures he likes—from
leaving for the winter, he finds himself in a battle with clever, crafty squirrels who want a share of the abundant food.

[1. Human-animal relationships—Fiction. 2. Squirrels—Fiction. 3. Old age—Fiction. 4. Birds—Fiction.
5. Humorous stories.] I. Salmieri, Daniel, 1983– ill. II. Title.
PZ7.R83116Tho 2008
[E]—dc22
2007040110

ISBN 978-0-547-00703-8 hardcover
ISBN 978-0-547-57681-7 paperback

Manufactured in China
SCP 10 9

4500526947

On the outskirts of town, at the edge of the forest, there was a little old house. The only thing older than the little house was the man who lived in it: Old Man Fookwire.

Old Man Fookwire was so old that when he sneezed, dust came out. He was also a grump.

He hated pie.

He hated puppies.

The only thing he liked was birds.

All summer long, the old man painted pictures of the birds that visited his backyard. There were whirley birds and bonga birds, baba birds and yaba birds. Even a rare floogle bird came by once or twice.

Fookwire's paintings weren't very good, but the birds never said anything.

When the air turned crisp and the leaves began
to change color, the old man grew sad. He knew that
soon the birds would fly south for the winter, as they
did every year, and that he would be lonely.

Then he had an idea: If he fed the birds, maybe
they would stick around.

So Old Man Fookwire built beautiful birdfeeders and put them up all around his backyard. He filled the feeders with delicious seeds and berries, and soon birds came from all over the forest just to eat in the old man's yard.

But the birds weren't the only ones who liked the birdfeeders. The squirrels did, too.

Not many people know this, but squirrels are the cleverest of all the woodland creatures. In fact, they're fuzzy little geniuses! They can make a house out of a tree,

a bed out of a bunch of leaves, and a box kite out of twigs, dirt, and squirrel spit.

They are also excellent at math.

Winter was fast approaching, and the squirrels needed to gather as much food as they could to get ready. So they decided to take some of the bird food.

The birds were not happy.

Neither was Old Man Fookwire. When he discovered what had happened, he shook his old man fist and yelled, "Those darn squirrels!"

He filled up the feeders again, but this time he hung them from a clothesline. Then he went back inside, confident that the squirrels would no longer be able to get to the seeds and berries.

But the squirrels were determined.
They devised a plan, and this time they
took *all* the food from the birdfeeders.

The birds were furious. *"Harrumph! Harrumph! Harrumph!"* yelled a bonga bird.

"Those darn squirrels!" yelled old man Fookwire.

"Yum!" said the squirrels.

Now it was Old Man Fookwire's turn to devise a plan. He went to the general store to get supplies. He bought lasers and clamps. He bought wires and springs. He bought all sorts of tools and built a veritable fortress around his birdfeeders.

Then he refilled them. Very carefully.

"Nah, nah, nah, nah, nah!" snorted the floogle bird.

The squirrels stayed up all night working out their strategy. They drank cherry cola and ate salt-and-vinegar chips to help them stay awake. Finally, they had it: the perfect plan!

They put on their tiny helmets and prepared to launch themselves into the air, over the fence, between the lasers, and onto the birdfeeders.

The first squirrel
misfired and hit a tree.

The second squirrel went too
high and landed in a bucket.

The third squirrel sailed
clear over the house.

The birds laughed and laughed. They each had one last delicious mouthful of seeds and berries from the old man's feeders. Then they flew south for the winter—just as they did every year.

"*Thhbbbtz!*" said the floogle bird.

After the birds left, Old Man Fookwire was lonely, just as he was every year. He fixed himself some cottage cheese and pepper—his favorite snack—but he was still lonely. When he looked out the window, the squirrels could tell that he wasn't happy.

"Go away!" shouted the old man. "I don't like you squirrels!"

The squirrels held a meeting deep inside a large tree. They decided to give the old man a present to make up for taking the seeds and berries.

Squirrel Meeting Tonight

Now, not many people know this, but squirrels are not only fuzzy little geniuses, they also collect just about anything they find on the ground. These squirrels had a vast stockpile of spectacular junk to choose from. But what would Fookwire like? Bottle caps? Popsicle sticks? Postage stamps? Finally, they had it: the perfect gift!

The squirrels stacked all of their loose change on Old Man Fookwire's doorstep. There were dimes and pennies. There were nickels and quarters. There were even a few tokens from Koko's Arcade. It all added up to forty-seven dollars and thirty-six cents—plus a few rounds of Skee-Ball.

"Maybe you squirrels aren't so bad," Fookwire said when he found the coins. "But I still like birds better!"

This gave the squirrels *another* idea. They raided their junk collection again and got to work.

When Old Man Fookwire woke up the next morning,
he was amazed to see that the birds had returned.

But wait! Those things weren't birds. They were squirrels in disguise!

"Great googley-moogley!" said Old Man Fookwire. "This will make quite a painting!"

He ran outside and took down the lasers and the wires and the spring-loaded trapeze. He turned all the birdfeeders into squirrel feeders. Then he painted till his brush ran out of bristles.

The squirrels were so overjoyed, they had a party . . . in Old Man Fookwire's house. "Those darn squirrels," said Fookwire, and he shook his old man fist and smiled.